THE EYES OF CONTRNELLE
A NOVEL

Masonia Williams

authorHOUSE®

AuthorHouse™
1663 Liberty Drive
Bloomington, IN 47403
www.authorhouse.com
Phone: 1 (800) 839-8640

Published by AuthorHouse 12/13/2017

ISBN: 978-1-5462-1775-6 (sc)
ISBN: 978-1-5462-1774-9 (e)

Library of Congress Control Number: 2017917661

Print information available on the last page.

Any people depicted in stock imagery provided by Thinkstock are models,
and such images are being used for illustrative purposes only.
Certain stock imagery © Thinkstock.

This book is printed on acid-free paper.

Because of the dynamic nature of the Internet, any web addresses or links contained in
this book may have changed since publication and may no longer be valid. The views
expressed in this work are solely those of the author and do not necessarily reflect the
views of the publisher, and the publisher hereby disclaims any responsibility for them.

Pounelle England former 2 year champion of Derby International was called to face her fears and conquer them by receiving and accepting her destiny by helping the most ebony beauty that the world is afraid of accepting, Contrnelle England. As Pounelle and Contrnelle goes into this unbelievable journey and meet the opponents that will do anything to kill the dreams that Pounelle will do to make the world remember her as the daughter of the Champions, not the vengeance of fear.

INTRODUCTION

The Eyes of Contrnelle A Novel

The sun raised and wind blew while the stallion horse's came running through the cold, lightful water splashing their feet and passing the trees (Pounelle). Ever looked into the horse's eyes and find the look of fierceness, boldness and keen. An opportunity of its own chance, to take risks or to give wildness a second look of its nature, to face reality into a sign into spiritual being of being different. Different is a sign of a different color when something is not respected of culture or not given cause of its own thought. A horse is a horse, a heart of a king and an a champion of a ring. People say a champion is a good sport but I say a champion soars through pain and caps through her own passion and ready to go to her destiny and laugh out every detail. Welcoming is a challenge but becoming has just began.

CHAPTER 1

Silence was the key to all notes when I walked in the room. I turned to my right side and seen Contrnelle running in the dark shadows eyes fearfully steady on me, black fur shining like Glossary Coats, sound of footsteps sounded like million horses. My heart pounding, my mind wondering into different turns. Imagination running wild into waterfalls and stallion horses running as a unit. As I get on and whispers Destiny ready to go. Contrnelle runs out the born at mid-morning sky turning grey and ready to rain. Finally, God decided to let rain and Contrnelle to a picture of Destiny in birds wings. It felt like Eagles of wings. 5 to 6 eagles flying in circles. The horse gets over powered and shows off a lot of dirt. Mud splashing on black fur and on me. Into the 1,860 acres of fields we go, into trees and bushes. Runway was in the middle and Contrnelle did not stop panting to get to Destiny 2. Rain kept on coming and coming and did not stop. Mom did not know I was riding Contrnelle for 3 months now and it will be ashock for mom but Contrnelle has not been touched ever since we won the 2 year Derby and ran against Castle and got into second place. Down a slippy hill we go but Contrnelle held her pace and went downhill without having second thoughts. I held the horses collar back so we wouldn't go down hill but boldness took over fear and fear was not part of Destiny 3. I can hear her heart racing and pounding but I can hear my pulse go 180 and mind going to 890 in thinking. We came back to our castle and to the barn we go to. Contrnelle jogs when she hears my name being called by my youngest brother Noah England that is barely 3 years old and very annoying. I ran towards my brother and in the house into the first door, holding my horse's shoes in my hand with wet clothes, when I saw mom come out of her room with a luxury sleepwear and a rob on. I runs into the room taking off my pants, throwing wet shoes in the closet and hitting the showers. Pounelle! My mom says gentle with a grin. By the time she got in I was out the shower dying my hair with Aloxxi hair dye, applying the towel to my damped hair. After I picked out my outfit that I already laid out to wear in the bathroom and then I applied my lip color pink, nude eye shadow, red blush, and mascara with blue eyeliner, fixing my new hair color red in place of all red, red and black colors then looks in the marble floor that was in her own bathroom. She walks to her Ethan Allen stool chair and looks inside her drawer and got her a led pencil and her dairy out that she plans out for Contrnelle and wrote down her plan for Contrnelle and her. While a certain song was on Deva Premal was playing inside the speaker in my bathroom and my room, I felt at peace on my stool dropping my pencil and I was zapped. The door knocks and I finally woke up feeling not strong at all. Pounelle! I heard my name clear as day but nothing was right in my mother's voice that was sweet.

CHAPTER 2

Fully awake when I heard my mother's voice. Two knocks pounded on the door. My mind started to wonder closely to the door as it kept pounding and pounding. I finally opened the door as it had up to five knocks on the door. Mother standing next to the door with a belt in her hand. I didn't even show no fear to open, I glanced as I opened the door and walked back to my stool, picked up my diary and pencil and put it by the drawer. Pounelle sighs and then looked at her mother. Yes, Mama? No answer but a share of disappointment. Have you,,, my mother freezes with my words, rain hits the house roof hard as my mom confronting me about Contrnelle. Have you been riding Contrnelle behind my back? Proselluia asked with her arms folded giving me a mom look. Have you? Yes, I have been for three months, mother gave a scoff throwing her two arms in the air. Great, Great, Great! So, not telling me is a great term for a 15 year old daughter. I am very surprised at you, I really am, Why? I asked in anger, I decided for me, I didn't consult you, Is that what you mad at? Always jumping to conclusions and not waiting for the unexpected to come along. You are becoming something that you are not. Mom, Interrupted. How can you say that? Finally, your daughter is doing something she loves. Maintaining freedom, love and becoming bold and enjoying your world that you created. Creation is being you but having a different being of you. Mom, you had went into our world and you have seen the society of worlds and its changing, what is it changing for? Is it for the people, their lives so people can be happy or is it changing for evil, the worst, hate and not excepting people to be them and not excepting freedom of others that has everything and this everything may change this world around by having one horse with pride and dignity and self respect, confident enough to give this world all she got with a heart full soul, rising up and taking a stand, just taking a stand, mama. Pounelle, you are not riding anymore. I'm sorry but you have lost that right. Mama, Dad is always against your say about Contrnelle. He won't go against my say about this one. Well, I'm sorry that you feel that way but I made my decision. I am riding Contrnelle and I will become the best of it. You're done, Pounelle. You're done. A slight grin came on my face as I glanced at my mother. Seem like the woman society does not have you as Ambassador of Chicago. What? What are you saying? Asked my mother? You know exactly what I am saying, you have always had a heart for children and the for the homeless. They have Emma Chellsa as Owner and Charlie Emila as Ambassador. Mom shifts her eyes on the marble floor and look up to the ceiling with tears in her eyes. Mom walks ou the bathroom sniffing her tears back, walking slow down the hall way. Pounelle's father Bicklen comes out and clears his throat and gives Proselluia a dirty look. He grabs his suit jacket with a newspaper in his hand. 846 million down the drain and an new face of company that belongs to the England Family.

CHAPTER 3

A flight to Chicago was occurring on the 4:55pm plane. Proselluia England enjoy your flight. A seat on First Class. Wine? No, thank you. Please buckle up your seat belts and enjoy your flight. A 4 day flight to Chicago. Welcome to Chicago Airlines, place your bag right here so we can do security check, thank you. Phone rings and Noah answers, Hello, mommie! Hello, baby! Is your father there? Yep, he is. Love ya. Love you too. I'm here in Chicago already. How is Pounelle? Their was no answer. Is that It? You still didn't answer my question. Bye, Proselluia. That evening Pounelle was out at the farm with Contrnelle shining her black coat with water. An old man came toward her with an cone to help him walk. He clears his throat, Um, My name is Johnton Castle, I am Amelia Castle's uncle. She never met me, Pounelle. Pounelle England and this is my horse Contrnelle England, I am kin to the England Family, yes. She says as she walked out of Contrnelle's section onto the grass they go, Oh, by the American's stories is-Stop! Stop! I'm not here to talk about the British Colonies. I am sorry for being so rude but your services are not in good shape. My investments built this from bottom to top and here are the papers to prove it. My signature is at the top, but I don't know about now, cause some women's society. Proselluia England wants to help the hungry children grow from hunger. I'm sorry, I am not the type of- Are you okay, Mr. Castle? Oh honey don't worry I express my anger to people all the time. Uh, while we at it, let's talk business. After I ride Contrnelle. People say that Castle can beat Contrnelle but Contrnelle has heart and soul. How can you manage a horse that way? Asked Mr. Castle? Pounelle chuckled. It must be grace and pride. This is not about winning a horse race, this is about showing the world about living in will of freedom.

By the time Jon got to Pounelle it was sunset and it was on great tasks. Jon tsks tsks at his horse as he was coming down hill as Pounelle and Contrnelle third eye grows strong as one they were still at their moment. Jon arrives and Pounelle sighs and turns to Jon's way. Jon walks more fast to her, he kneels down and as he kneels down Contrnelle follows suits. I want you to win but follow your heart and let Contrnelle lead. Contrnelle agree to the term that he was saying. Would you be my life? Show me what you are all about. I want you...as he pauses, as he put the ring on her third finger. Contrnelle bumped into her and Pounelle's answer came out Yes. A laugh came out with a cough. Contrnelle runs while Jon and Pounelle was hugging tightly with filled hearts.

CHAPTER 4

When Derbey's lead owner came to our front gate it was a shock, cause derbey final was at the door waiting to be knocked over to turn. Hello Mr. Ayes, a shock fever came over me, like cold water with cold pencils as I walked down the stairs to meet him. I was introduce to a 6'2 260 tall man that was bigger than daddy. Pounelle England, Willton Ayes, nice to meet you! Please come in, Thank you, Mr. Ayes says as he came in looking at the trophies Contrnelle won. Is this you and Contrnelle? Yes it is, 460 grand to ride Contrnelle again if you can beat your opponent each week or each month at each palace. If you win 460 grand to you and to your investor 286 grand out of your 460 grand. So, what do you say? Where is the contract? Here it is all in one, take your time, read the fine print, Mr. Ayes says as he looks at her and smiles but eyes are fiercely on her. Pounelle's flashback at the crown cheering Contrnelle as she runs her race. Are you okay? Mr. Ayes says with his african accent being concerned coming up and touching her shoulder. Are you - Bicklen interrupted as he was coming towards the stairs with his back turned to the chinas drawings. Dad, Pounelle says as she walks towards him with a low grin. Pounelle, this is your life, your decision and I'm there for you, you don't need permission to do you, you got money, youare grown enough to take care of yourself.

A lot of 15 year olds wished they would have the gut to take risks that you are about to take, just be you and be happy says her dad. Hello, Bicklen England. What do I have to do to these forms? I have someone I want you to meet, someone special that you never met. Dad opens the door to the bedroom and cand cough as we opened the door. The older woman that was in the guest room was in the bed, holding her hands up to shake Pounelle's hands. Dad, did not say a thing just looked and had tears moving slowly on his face, heart and tears was in emotion. Crying all week long. Who is this? Pounelle asked with low speech, your Godmother, she raised you and Contrnelle when me and your mother was in Africa saving hungry children. A flashback came to Pounelle as she held on to her Godmother Emma's hand as tight as she could, while her memory of her and emma playing. I am so proud of you, Emmas says I'll almost to her last breath. You win cause you are a woman of your own confidence and say yes to that boy he seems ready for committment. A gasp came into her last say. I sighs as I closed her eyelids with my two fingers. Rest in peace, my friend, rest in peace. Daddy tsks as he silently cries. Pounelle walks slowly towards her father and as she grabs the door knob and finally walks out.

CHAPTER 5

(Pounelle) This is the time I say to be free of Society and shame, this is the time for Contrnelle and I to find out our honest selves. When times got rough after all Contrnelle did have her wonders at chances. Standing in front of a casket and look in front of it and it is staring you in the face, nothing can be taken including your pride and faith in God put in front of you. A beautiful quote was said upon me, "you will always have the say of your day". I looks at the sign of when she died 1901-2027, 126 lives she lived and now she finally lived until this day. Her spirit still lives and her soul willb e kept into our heart. I rose my head as I seen Jon at the funeral bowing his head at me. A wind blows while Contrnelle was at the top of the hill by the setting sunset, bowing down to the sadness that came to the England Family. While Pounelle was staring at her mother, Jon came behind and put his hand on her right shoulder. When the funeral was over, Jon pulled Pounelle to the side and said, "Contrnelle is waiting for you, just be you, be you." Jon says as he holds her hand, runs through the crowd that was at the funeral. Contrnelle runs to them and Pounelle rides him as fast as she could, running towards the sunset. A blossom came to a point in the hearts of the ebony stallion horse was conquering her art of living. Becoming free of fear and flying all up and above, running wild in the mind of your own imagination, to be considerd thoughtless among others, but to remember what you are fighting for, it is the key of proving insanity wrong.

CHAPTER 6

AFRICA

Contrnelle was happy to bring excitement and joy to the children. Africa was where she was raised and honored where she was admired. Children shouting Contrnelle cheering her name, bringing back the crown of the derby palace, hearing the name and putting it all in one glory. Children of Africa was surrounding Pounelle, holding my hand and making me feel welcome in thier home, in tradition of wealth and riches. It was an honor to see Contrnelle bowing her head to the children and letting them get a ride. I chuckles and smiles as Contrnelle had a grin on her face. A necklace was place on my neck, I felt my heart burning with the desire to love and be free, fire of heartwhelming came inbetween, pulses moving quickly everywhere in body. I glance at the children cheering and cheering heart beating. A hand grabs me but my mind was not paying attention, my eyes wonders to the black sky, the reflection in task. Pounelle! Pounelle look, look! my eyes and body moves to the direction they were pointing to. Jon standing in position and smiling to the connection that was made before them. Jon runs to her and hugs her. What? I drove 155 hours and 6,942.1 miles to love you, to motivate you and cherish you with one sound mind. If you let me, I can be your shining armor. Pounelle laughs and nods her heard. Contrnelle neighs to them as she bows in the middle of them. The village cheers as they share a simple kiss as it rains for the third time Pounelle, Contrnelle and Jon stayed and laughed and praised their moment together. Be Free, Jon whispered, be free, Jon whispered again. Come. Lets go. In the village shed they go into. A man was in the middle of the floor, legs crossed. Oh, come on in, my children. Are you ready to be the wife of Jon Gloryson Eagleton? Pounelle, freezes gentle as she looked shocked. You Ok? Jon asked. Gloryson Eagleton is your two middle names? Pounelle sighs gently asking. Yes, it is. Have we been married before? Pounelle says breathless. Yes, but not by our own personal will. You two are meant for each other. I know, Pounelle says, sighing. My name is Joseph and this is my son. I am Gloryson Eagleton, Joseph Gloryson Eagleton, and its a pleasure to meet you Mrs. Eagleton. Um..we are not married yet." Well, indeed you are still married legally to Mrs. Eagleton. Wait, it can't be, Pounelle says as she yells across the village. But it is, so let it be. Honey, let's go back inside. Alright, Pounelle agreeed, without fussing. How long have we been married? Pounelle asked, calmly as she could bare. 7 years, that's how long we have been married? 7 years? Wow, ever since we were 9, at the time arranged marriages had occurred in China. If my parents find out this..Pounelle pauses, don't worry, sooner or later they are going to have to let it go, cause they agreed and I have agreed to love and honor you, and to motivate you and to pray for you. Oh, honey, I love you. Wedding planning! Child Yells! Pounelle looks at the 2 wedding rings that was on her fingers, Jon? Yes, what is it? You got me two rings instead of one? No wonder all of those years, 7 years, I never took off this lovely ring. What? You never took off your ring? Never. Music plays and plays for Pounelle and Jon. Here in Africa we celebrate by kissing other's hand, like this. Its a greeting and this is for you. Thank you! You're welcome! I sighs and looks at Jon and smiles. I am with you all the way. When the greetings last out all night long. Jon and Pounelle was at the Niagara waters with Contrnelle and Gabriel just relaxing and having a wonderful experience. I love you! Jon looks deeply in her eyes and gives her a deep kiss and says, "Do you love you? and I am not talking about loving you. Are you loving the destiny that is inside of you? Pounelle, Do you really want this?" Do you? I...Yes, I do. Good, Jon says as he was holding Pounelle's hand, walking towards the center of the water. The center of it was our connection Jon finally heard stallions running closely together, Contrnelle finally neighs up to praise attention. Other white stallions stopped and sighs. Contrnelle walks through the middle of the line and cuts through and gave a fearless look. The expression gave, I'm ready to ride look. My eyes lifted from the water to Contrnelle. Close and personal Contrnelle was ready, Contrnelle rises Pounelle's chin up gently and looks upon.

CHAPTER 7

Pounelle and Jon to downtown England on a private boat for 4-7 days straight. Jon pulled up to the rail where two men was chatting. Hello Miss Pounelle, she nods, Contrnelle was there first at the rail waiting at England downtown. Jon arrives behind Pounelle and asks her, where do I put these? right over by my wagon. Pounelle stops at the news stand and sees her mother's picture about the Women's Society. You can't trust no one can you now these days, can you? A voice came behind her. Pounelle glances over her left shoulder, do I know you? I'm sorry, where are my manners? I am Mrs. Bulluaton, Chelsa Bulluaton, and yours? Pounelle England Eagleton, Mrs. Eagleton, oh, nice to meet you. They are so cruel aren't they? asked Mrs. Bulluaton. Sorry, how old are you? asked Pounelle. What difference does it make, we are both married women right? Pounelle chuckles, softly, I guess we are. I am 17 and you? Oh, I'm 15. Wow how delightful, and old people say we are too yound. In my fact of state, they forget how that used to be when they were young. Oh, this is my husband, Jon Eagleton. Oh, how wonderful, I hope you can stay for a cup of tea? Yeah, I would be honored. Please, follow me, Mrs. Bulluaton says, as we were going into her home. Does anyone live with you? Pounelle asks. Nope, just me, my husband, and my son. Wow, Mrs. Bulluaton this is nice. So, Pounelle, how long have you been married? 7 years, hm, no wonder you both are strongly rightful. Thank you, Pounelle and Jon said together. 12 years, that is how long I have been married. Now these days old people get married and stay for so long 50,60 years, and still stay together. So, I want the same thing and so, here I am. I am happy. We don't get in arguments that much like we should, we communicate but there are no arguments. My first husband died in the war of saving children, and now I have...Chelsa stops and turns around, her father, Mr. Ayes comes in the dinner room, drinking his whiskey in a mini bar shot glass. Uh, Father? Pounelle? Well, what a beautiful surprise. I am glad you met my daughter Chelsa. This is a great place to talk business. Meet 2 year champion Pounelle England, Pounelle England, meet 5 year champion Chelsa Ayes Bulluaton. Meet her attorney and Dr. Asol Bulluaton, her husband. Hi, Hi how are you? Now, I have made it official that this is your opponent for 3 years in a row from 2026-2029, this will be your opponent. Bets will be made and it is your job to keep your priorities up. Do we understand? Yes. Two women says out loud. Great, sign! Jon Interrupted, Asol looked surprised and moved closer to Chelsa. Jon held eyes with Asol. We will do this at a later date. You don't have no say! Asol yells out. Chelsa taps her husband's chest, babe, let it go. She has a choice like us. Pardon me? Yeah, keep doing your sissy technique, Jon says, as he gently grabs Pounelle. Bye, Burger King. Pounelle says back with a smile back at Chelsa. Chelsa was at the expression was not kind nor polite. Miss England do you want anything. Uh, yes, please, bring me hotdogs, cornbread, chicken feet, ham and please bbq, and some fries. Oh, come on Jon, we don't have time. What you mean, we don't have time. Jon mickied. You mean you don't have time...I don't know who you talking to. Jon says as he makes a scen in public heading out the door, trying not to go but being shoved out the door. Wait a second! Let me get my shoes on, Jon shutters out the door. Oh, my God.

The butler finally comes in with the order, what is this? You ordered hot dogs, cornbread, and chicken feet, ham, bbq and some fries, Sir, he grabbed the plate and started to eat. Jon and Pounelle drove away in their wagon. I don't trust em, Pounelle. What? All of a certain she just came out about Mr. Ayes about being head boss? I guess. Pounelle answered. Grow up. Jon replied. As they entered the hills they stopped in the middle of the land, where it said, "Private Property", Pounelle gasps, what is this? Jon smiles. Welcome to our new home! I have been building it for 2 years now, this is your home Contrnelle and the other stallions have their space and this land is ours! It has upstairs, kitchen, bathrooms, rooms, furniture, everything to have us a family house. 5 rooms and 6 bathrooms, water and mountains to look at, not too many 15 year olds can build something like this. Yeah you are right. So, when are you riding again? Pounelle, chuckles. Soon, its hard to tell, dad won't pay for anything, I have to be a woman now, I can't let insanity win over my power of winning. This is about me and Contrnelle now and how we are going to reach Destiny's. How can we not do it? My intentions are to overcome and prove people wrong. I already proved to myself that I am queen of my own life by winning the derby 2 times without hesitation and now it is time to prove to others about their instinct and insecurities are wrong. I am just trying to live my life, Jon. I am getting at that point now, I don't need boundaries to live my life. I am an Eagleton and I am ready to fly with eagles wings. I just want to live, Pounelle says with a smile, but with a fierce look.

Contrnelle runs freely into 642,000 acres she goes into. Jon and Pounelle smiles together as they embrace closer they get the closer she finds her main point of living. (Pounelle) There is no point of living if fear is in the way, the waking of independence has a theme of a song, if you so choose to listen. As a reminder, mountains speak and God claims what is his and this fierce beauty he put before thee has already mastered her own self – righteous. And so for thee has before me, love and destinies will be filled with generation hope for the mighty high and praise will be thy name, thou kingdom come.

CHAPTER 8

Contrnelle and Pounelle came from a long experience of desire. Proselluia ran to Pounelle and hugged her daughter tightly as she could bare. Hon, don't do that again! Where have you been? Who were you with? Pounelle sighs and looks on her bare shoulder. I have my own home mama, I was with Jon. You mean…that small little…Jon? Pounelle laughs, Yes, he is yours, What? Welle, he is married to your kin, me. Pounelle says as three Kings of Diamonds was on each finger, Three? He mom stutters her speech, Oh, no, he is not. Yes, he is mama, we been married for 7 years and believe me, ma, it was a shock. Do you love him? Contrnelle loves him, she cuddles up to him when she wants attention. See! Pounelle shows her photos. Contrnelle bows down to Proselluia and nods. Does your dad know about this? Of course he do. Uh-huh, yeah. Bicklen, her father pulls up in front of the house. Bicklen! Yes! Who gave her permission? Ohh, some rings I hope it the one you got married before to. Bicklen and Pounelle shared nose kisses. Ameliaty England, Pounelle's Grandmother came in with the news paper. Contrnelle is Fraud! And it is asking for 200 pounds. Jon pulls up with a sack of two in his, everyone else went inside leaving them alone on porch. Jon? I heard what is going on and I know what I need to do for you, you are going to get on that horse and you going to win. I sold everything, the jewelry store, the art gallery for you, my darling little lamb. Her is 500 pounds, I can get the gallery back, I can get everything back, from my uncle, this is for you darling. You are my love, I put all my dreams aside for you, I don't care about how much you make, you just run your race!

CHAPTER 9

Sighs came along for all girl derbey. I sighs and look at the girls as they were standing around waiting for the next person to get out of line, two more people came out of line and Pounelle was next in line to sign. Name: the man asked harshly with a look of inpatience, Pounelle England, Champion? Excuse me? Are you still Champion? Former Champion, he nugged the pen to former. Age: 15 Month May 11, Year 2012. Excellent, your agency contract is Jon Eagleton. You will be getting 476,000 per race each month and you will pay have of that 476,000, put your bags on the bus. Pounelle, your mother called. I am with you on this one. You just win your race and bring home that title! Do you hear me?! Yes mama, I hear you. Love you! Pounelle steps on the bus and sits in the front row. Multiple of girls joined and got on the bus. Hi, do you mind if I sit here? Oh of course not, Pounelle says with a low grin. Celsavenia. Pounelle England. Oh, cute, are you from her? Um yes, lived here ever since, how old are you? Celsa asked with a smirk of grace, I'm 15 and you? 39. Are you married? Uh, yes, children? Yes, I never seen before, in a matter of face here is a photo of him and a girl that looks familiar. Pounelle looked harshly into the photo fiercely. Celsa looked and Pounelle glances at each other's rings and necklaces. Some kind of rings and necklaces were the same, two children in China komos dresses, one woman style and boy style with dragon tail in the back. Pounelle pounds more as the bus starts to move. No more seats are available at this time. Gotta wait until next year, says the driver! Chatters in the back of the bus. (Pounelle) My mind starts to wonder strongly about that photo about things that I didn't know. Everything didn't seem right. A person naked came to mind. Death was coming to someone close to someone's heart. This derbey didn't find attractive. Celsa felt nervous, I felt hardly outspoken and ready to fight of what is mines 2 years. I waited for this moment and it is finally here. Let everything come hardly into this derby. I am ready, stronger, and faster. So let's hold our hands together and pray for a miracle to happen.

CHAPTER 10

AWAY FROM HOME

As the derby queens arrived to Kansas Palace, the queens were about to be sports illustrated all over news. Pounelle looks straight to castle's opponent, Klemnta Greece. Stay out of my way! Or what? Pounelle answered eye to eye. Oh, no, I want to know, since you are the one with the mouth. Does you dad know you have a big mouth cause when I get done with ya, you are going home with no money for the next year. Keep on you may find yourself a slink says Greece. Pounelle chuckles, you keep on you may find yourself getting a punch in the face with your round two bullet across your neck, and all you may have is my name across your back. Pounelle says with a smirk. Pounelle England the man started calling names, Klemnta Greece, Blen Contaya, Chelsa Bulluaton, and Lena Linulla. Please step forward, come this way please. They came forth and walked in as a clutter. Pounelle England? Please this way, all of them split 5 ways into a star. I went straight to the room they wanted me in with a camer to my face. Hello, please have a seat, I'm Micheally Sprinfield, I will be asking all the questions from time to time, Uh, How does it feel to be away from home? Pounelle: "it feels great, it just a new beginning for me, but I am really excited to go around the world again and see many things and it feels exciting to be away, but lonely for mama's sweet cornbread". Reporter: What inspired you to do something like this? Pounelle: I don't know I just have a lot to be, this is my favorite season and I just want to be Champion again, cause I know I can beat that timer when the horse is steady, she's ready to run. Reporter; Oh yeah, Ok, Next question: Do you feel threatened by your other opponents that have more experience than you? Pounelle: Uh, I don't feel threatened by anyone, but I think some are threatened by me. I really don't care about experienced people. I am just as good as they are. Reporter: Last question, How do you feel about Jon Eagleton being President of the Derbey? Pounelle: Jon Gabrielton Eagleton? I think he can make the derbey run for their money and keep the business head of town. He is a great source and he is made to be president. That was great, cut. Wow, that was great, Mama's Cornbread" I can just taste that on the tip of my tongue says Micheally the reporter says with a cup of chicken soup in his hand. "cornbread with greens, black eyed peas and some bbq chicken, whoo! Thank ya! Micheally says with a hand praising. So, what do you think? Pounelle was gone as he looked up, where did you go? Jon waiting outside with a 7000 pay check. Mr. Eagleton, Mrs. Eagleton, Shh, stop it! Here is your payecheck and everytime you do those interviews you will be paid. $7000 per interview, $482,360 per conference room, $432,682 per room and I will keep your books you get my meaning? Yes, I get your meaning. Mr. Eagleton says Pounelle with a sharp edge tone.

CHAPTER 11

Derbey's divas were all there in the conference sitting in the cold air conditioning, hmm, it is cold in here, I wonder is it cause the wonder queen? Keep pushing, Pounelle says, with a smile. You two stop it! We got three weeks before the derbey and I am not going to have you two fucking it up for all of us, when two people make mistakes, they have all of us cleaning it up, says Linulla. Linulla says, talking to Greece. Reporters came in finding their seats and taking their pictures. Pounelle? Are you ready for the derbey? If you ask me I think I am ready. Greece interferes in the question of Pounelle, think meaning- uncertain and unsure, and if you get in the field with me, you better be sure. The reporters laughed with joy but Greece did not like the manners that held before her. The other four couldn't get a word out because Greece was talking and Pounelle was answering boldly. Reporter: Does your horse have any speed like Contrnelle? Greece: for being an 6 year champion, my horse has the most speed. Reporter: Pounelle? Pounelle: and my horse has the most heart, you have to have a strong heart to run the derbey race. Greece: anybody can see that your horse is no use, Pounelle: and anybody can see that you don't have the bold gut to come say it to my face. Greece: fine, I can beat you, just tell me what time. Pounelle: right now! Greece:

bring it! Pounelle: Anytime! Pounelle finally takes the punch first one time in the face and two time on the side and an double kick from Pounelle. Security came out and got both of them outta there. As the security guard held them both straight, and before you knew it, Greece's hair was pulled by Pounelle. I have it covered, Jon says outside to Asol Enough! Asol yells! Take them away! What operation are you running here? Ladies and Gentlemen, please forgive this incident, that you have seen here tonight, No questions tonight please, enjoy your eveing. Jon says soothing and peaceful. Asol: Pounelle is so ungrateful. Jon looks at him and socks him one time in the nose. Jon: If you ever talk about my wife again I will kill you. Pounelle! Jon shouted, You alright, is she alright? Greece added. If you ever pull that stunt again in my conference room, Greece, you would never again. Greece started everything. Greece? Asol started to come in yelling at Jon with a bloody patch over his nose. Who do you think you are? Asol says in temper anger. A man that is in charge that your father left to me and if I am around, you are going to answer to me, or you can kiss you 946,762,000 dollars away for touching the CEO and say goodbye to that Gucci that, Louis Vuiton, and that Odce Galbana expense and go back to that poor life. Jon said in fast pace. Jon: did you get that? Asol: Are you threatening me boy? Jon: Boy? Hmm, that's clever but a boy? You're only 17 and I am only 15 but I know reputation and a person, that brings age up into the conversation has no opinion to the money I have. People don't ask me how old I am or how are you doing at business. They know I can take everything they have just for asking. Asol: This is the only job I can get that pays good quality money. My uncle black bald me for making us lose everything. Jon: Then you better with the program and don't ever talk about my wife again or I will give you more than a bloody nose. And you two girls, get ready for the match race cause in a couple of hours, cameras will be on the person that will win, and be in the derbey. Here are the rules:

1. No cheating whoever cheats will never get to race three weeks from now. You wait 6 years before racing again.
2. The score will be 5:46 if you beat the timer before 14:26 then you will win and go around the world. 3. If you tie, both of you will complet the signs of record. Contrnelle vs Castle in 4 in 1 odds. You two will go around fields and if it 5:45 you will lose the $46,802 thousand. And that is for all of you. Both of you will go around the track and run around bucket and go be to your chambers and your numbers are: Pounelle, 5, Greece 2, and if one of you win, one of you have to go. Those are my rules. Jon says. Your scouts will decide. You on the field.

CHAPTER 12

Contrnelle is the winner the Scotts decided to make when they seen Pounelle ride after hours, they knew the soar of a beauty will conquer it all in one state. Here are your contracts! Jon stated excited! Greece lowly read the contrace and it said exactly the same thing. Jon finally touches the bare skin of Pounelle's slightly Pounelle glances at him and smiles. Jon whispered, I love you! Here! Greece says, there you! Pounelle says second. Alright, girls you know what you have to do Pounelle, your 5 Greece, your 7. Jon added as he was walking towards the second step of the seats. 5:45 is score 5:46 time 20:20 and Go! All horses feet rumbled as they were running, Castle getting tired all ready and it have been 5 mins into the reace. Timere 19:40, 19:34, 19:30, 19:19, 19:14, Jon was keeping count out loud Contrnelle! Use your heart to keep, you got this you will be passed Destiny's number 3. This is Destiney 3. So, Con, Con, Let's go! (Jon) I pray that Contrnelle will win this race. I just want her to win and be free. I humbly thank you. Celsa was sitting one step on bleachers. Jon turns around and looks at her closely and turns back to the timer. Everybody was praying for Contrnelle and Pounelle to get it. Pounelle was in the lead with 50 points, Jon yells 5 more seconds. Pounelle glances at watch 10:04, 10:00, 9:50, Pounelle says loudly, you got it Con! (Pounelle) Her heart hears the crowd, her heart's steady the passion that is within thee. Her heart stands gently to the voice that she cater's to. Pounelle beat the time 5:45, 5:47 is one when she made it in. Greece was last. Pounelle, finally runs to her gate 5. Contrnelle heart was filled with joy, and Pounelle's fierce record was on the charts.

CHAPTER 13

NO EVIL SHALL COME BETWEEN US

Celsa Venia, Pounelle England, Klemnta Greece, Blena Contaya, and Chelsa Bulluaton, these are your new contenders, Mr. Ayes, Amelia Yan-China 20 year champion, Victorayan King- Asia 19 year champion. Pounelle and Celsa didn't even looked surprised. 32 years of riding. Celsa says. I would be glad to race. Let's do it then. These people mean business and they don't play, Celsa. I'm going to my room and rest for a while, Pounelle smiles at the beauty this is right in front. Hey Con! Bring you're a-game, someone is going to die tonight and I don't know who. Amelia staring at Pounelle and Contrnelle, but Pounelle didn't even move a stunt. Walks up to the stallion and looked at the other opponents eyes. Only thing was Amelia was the only one punking out. Pounelle: what, can't keep eye to eye contact? The 20 year champion chuckles. Pounelle: only a coward cheats, if anyone gets hurts, Mr. Ayes, I am kicking your ass, Pounelle says as she was walking away. Pounelle finally came in, Celsa sitting on the bed looking at a photo that Pounelle couldn't even understand. Your mail is on the table, thank you Celsa, you're welcome Pounelle. I'm going to take a shower, Ok, Celsa. Pounelle sits on Celsa's bed and looks at the photo Celsa's always cherished, and then the mail fell out of Pounelle's envelope. The same one photo Celsa had, Jon? Me? Pounelle says surprised. Dear Pounelle, it has been 4 months since we have not heard from you and Jon, your mother misses you and we will be there at the Derbey soon. At the end of not you will have $900 dollars cash. She looks through every mail, Jon and Pounelle same. Celsa was still in the shower. A knock came on the door, Jon had a puzzle look with photos in his hand. Pounelle didn't say a word. Did you get photos as well? Yes, Jon answered slowly, I couldn't look at them, it brought back thoughts of me and you. So, is Celsa's. Pounelle says as she game him Celsa's photo. Jon gasps and held down tears down but he could hold. So, she is my...Jon pauses through words your mother, Pounelle says with tears rolling down, Celsa finally came out, Mother? Jon asked, Slowly Celsa finally glances with teary eyes, Son? Celsa says with a smile, Yes Mom, Oh my God. They shared and embraced. After hours Derbey finally was starting people were bidding and children taking photos. Jon giving his mother Celsa one last hug, Jon watches his mother go into the crowd, people cheering, the expression on Celsa's face to strange death look. Numb hands and loose knuckles, every girl knows to their game that this is not a fair mark. Contender inside gates and ready to take head. Jon up in first class looking at Pounelle, but glances at his mother, Celsa, that was rider. Trumpet sound buzzes off, all horses go. Pounelle in the lead 70 point, Contaya is in the lead with 50 point, says the reporter. Celsa taken time with catching up. Now Contrnelle in the lead, leaving all over kind, crowd yelling for Contrnelle, but Celsa in the lead with 100 points, all she have to do is go as Eagle's opponent, Oh, my, Eagle and Celsa has won. The England stallion Eagle Venia has won this derbey. Ladies and Gentlemen, Celsa Venia has won the Derbey of England International. Ladies and Gentlemen Celsa Venia. Crowd cheering harder, Celsa glances at the top of glass, she nods and blows a kiss to her son, I love you Celsa says with her fist to her heart. Pounelle ran to Celsa, and hugs her, I am proud of you Celsa. I am too, darling Celsa put her hand on top of her chest as the crowds cheering get louder. Come on, Let's go get some water. Both of them went back to the water front and both drunk water. How does it feel to win first time in America? It feels awesome, I can feel the vibe inside of me… its just…celsa pauses again as she fall straight into Pounelle's arms, Celsa?! Pounelle yells out. My son! Jon comes towards Pounelle and bends down to hold her, I love my children, take care of yourself, Celsa's last breath was that. Dies in her son's arms. Jon whimpers as he cries softly to his mom's chest, Mama! Jon yells out softly. Then Jon finally waited and waited for the ambulance to come, and they came quickly, no blood showing, just a heart bursting out and ready to meet the heavenly father. Jon? I stated to call, but Jon hands pulled up the side and then waves and shakes not now, Pounelle, please, not now. Jon walks down the stairs and headed towards the front of the tracks. Jon sighs and looks up at the sky as rain started to poor down his face, no one at the derbey but Pounelle and Jon, chairs were empty, both of them were soaked and wet. Jon? I called out, Yes, Jon replied gentle, it thundered some more. Pounelle: you shared, laughed, and enjoyed each other and that's all that matters, nothing can take away that. Jon: Here is what I think? Show those bastards who is the Eagleton. I am been waiting all 4 months to do this. They shared a moment, and kissed. Pounelle: that is the best thing I ever had, you are so blessed. Jon: I am blessed to have you, I am thankful. Pounelle glances at Jon with a beautiful glance of love, Contrnelle finally runs out and greets them both. The bond of nature, it has many names of its own to say but to be risen and be fired already. I get the two mixed up. The next morning at 2 am, 3 am was a call to come to the conference. Differenct questions were asked before Jon, but Jon knew who set up the meeting. Mr. Ayes, sitting down smoking his cigar but all that changed with one hit on the lip. That same time it was different, Jon that was fearfully upright and more, than I expected. Expressions changed when Jon sat up at stand and looked dead at them in the eye: I stood in back of news casters as Jon was looking directly as me with all focus on me. How do you feel? Jon: What's your name? Reporter: Mahla Kaymlya. Jon: Asia? Reporter: Yes: Yes Asia. How did you know? Jon: your attention of status gave it all away. Reporter: Who was Celsa Venia? Jon: My mother! Celsa Venia was my mother: I was born in China, April 26, 2012, came back to England but first I was expectly raised in Africa where the mountains spoke, waterfalls of sound was all in affect. You can have love with desire there in Africa. Reporter: if You can't? Jon: If this, if that, there is no such thing, I can't. Everyone meet the woman that held my hand when my mother died, Pounelle Eagleton, Pounelle England Eagleton, that is my wife and she is going to be champion of this derbey, and I will be part owner.

Pounelle, my hon, you do whatever you need to do. You are different but with a smile. Pounelle smiles as she blows a kiss at him.

Ladies and Gentlemen please take a good look at your new derbey part owner. All I have to do is prove you all wrong. Reporter: You mean prove yourself? Jon: I married a wise queen that should tell you something. After many people tole me I couldn't guess what, I did. I proved to myself that I did, there where other fishes and rice, but why go out fishing, when you have the rice in your hand? I made the right choice and I love it.

Reporter: did you have many fishes? Jon: Yes, but one Fish, that was meant I looked straight into my one and only eyes and I knew then she was mine forever. The main objective is to stay focused and know what you want and mean it. That's it! No more questions. Jon that was great! Pounelle says as she held him close to her head. I am proud of you, I love you! Jon says as he looked inside her eyes. You are going to win. I believe you are and I know you do too. Just dream, fly and conquer it and become it. Get out of your way and run your race. Don't worry about me or our relationship, I will be here until you finish, just do what you need to do, if this company becomes ours, I mean part ours. Pounelle: you mean ours. Jon smiles and nods, Yes, Ours, you will be on the board with me. Pounelle: I want to prove this insanity badly, all my life I been told I can't. Jon: that's why are going to prove them wrong, you proved. Pounelle: to whom? Jon: your mother, Mr. Ayes, and this world, also Contrnelle proved that her legacy has just begun. The light was shinning as Pounelle walked closely to the door, in the middle of the tracks where it was froggy, Contrnelle running on the left side of the tracks, fur shinning as black as a beauty, Contrnelle, finally stops at her attention closely enough to her side shoulder as Pounelle looked on her left shoulder and imagined two riders coming to her but one horse in the middle of tracks down and not on its feet. I sighs, looking into the beautiful beauty that was right in front of me, are you ready for another ride? You, Contrnelle, this year's derbey is not a four tribe but we will show the world we are the name to us calling. Are you ready? Contrnelle touches the soft awaken skin and as she is awaken, she realizes the freedom they were close to, Pounelle sighs as she hears reporters in the background. Shh! Shh! Steady your desire! Steady! Steady! Steady! Pounelle says as she glances at Jon with paper and pen in his hand waiting for Pounelle to come. Here sign: Jon says as he gives Pounelle the black ink pen. For what? Pounelle reads the fine print of the contract, You're part owner of the International Derbey. I want to keep riding Contrnelle even if I am part owner, I don't want to be part owner, I want to be owner. Pounelle says as she looks at the pen with Jon's signature. Yes, Pounelle! I am sorry about your mother Jon, you okay? No answer came from Jon just tears but something edged Pounelle to sign those papers. Jon! Jon looked back quckly, Pounelle grabed wrote excitedly and bravely towards the paper

There...Yay! Pounelle says gently, but slowly, Contrnelle finally sleeps as Jon comes over and touches Con with his lovely passionate fingers whimpering and crying, Con? More crying came from Contrnelle, more tearing came from Contrnelle. Healing took place and hours and hours took plave was it the contract? Blank Contract! So, why is this one? You be surprised, they killed my mother slowly but the only that killed her was what she died for. Insanity and belief to find me. Jon! Jon! Jon! Reporters wants to see you! Pounelle! Reporter: when will the next derbey be? Jon: October 31, 2027. Reporter: Why on Halloween? Do you even have a clue that your workers will even be willing to show up, not having a chance to see families. What would happen? Jon: If they don't come in, they will lose commissions and pay. Reporter: like how much? Jon: like for daily income 482 million/commission 762 million. Reporter: why so much? Jon was about to talk, but the main owner came around the father of Ayes. Heart Ayes, Charles Heart Ayes the father of Jothan Ayes, but, was that his real name or was he hiding? Reporter: Mr. Ayes, as the reporters were shouting, Jon and Heart were mumbling. Heart: we need to talk, Jon:as you wish, both of them walked away and came to Jon Eagleton's office. Heart: What is this? Hey, this is my office. Jon: not anymore. Please Mr. Ayes, have a seat, take a load off your mind, Mr. Ayes, or shall I say Mr. Bulluaton. I can't tell which to call ya! Jon: Who are you? Mr. Ayes: No, No, No, young man, Who gave you these cautions to do this? Jon: Who gave you cautions to do this?! Speak English! Mr. Ayes: Who gave you authority? Jon: is your wife Amelia Eagleton? Did she help you build this derbey? Money marries money, huh? She is a rider right? Mr. Ayes: who caution? Jon: what is with these hard words you spitting, papa? Mr.

Ayes: What's wrong young blookd, can't keep up with an old spirit? Jon: You went to Oxford University? asked Jon as he pulled out the files of his record. Ain't nothing compared to mine, 4 yrs in China University, and 7yrs in England's University and graduated that same year. Mr. Ayes: where did you get this information? Jon: I did it for my wife, she wants her destiny filled, she got it. Now, my wife wants her name to be called and got that too. Now, I am here to make sure Pounelle England won't be treated any differently cause you are a stubborn old fool that can't be fair. Your wife and your son gave you up cause my Godfather Vent Stone died in front of my eyes, and handed over half of trillion of dollars in my name and all of this was my Godfather's idea and the only reason you stole my Godfather's idea is because you couldn't compete with a praying man, and that praying man loved your wife more than he loved his money and your wife became my Godmother. That's right, Mr. Ayes, my Godmother told me everything about you, Mr. Ayes and I am not pleased with the results. You been living off my Godfather for far too long. Mr. Ayes: So what does this mean? he says scared. Jon: You broke, Mr. Ayes, my Godfather would have done the same thing. I am the only child of Celsa Venia. You had the nerve to broadcast it in the news and papers that was not supposed to be but I guess it was. My Godmother took me to the mountains of China and told me to let life bring you. Mr. Ayes: I don't care about that. I want. Jon: Mr. Ayes, have you been listening? your wife Amelia and your son Jothan has signed a blank contract that made you lose everything. I own everything, your cars, your limo company, your 470 million pension, your $478,786,226,676,097.66 and more in the bank account that you thought no one knew about. Also including the people you ripped off they are with me on this one. You all willing to pay all your riders what they deserve, but I forget you already did. That blank contract that your son signed, this derbey belongs to my wife and me. All these 3 years since I been working for this derbey, I've been aggressively watching you live off my Godfather's living, you have nothing to stand on. Mr. Ayes: This is not over, you are going to rot for this. Jon: the judge will never cooperate, your name won't matter anymore and the reason why you have so much power is because of your name, and your money that you use to own to intimidate and get your way, but all of that is over, cause I am here and this is mine. My wife will reach her destiny thanks to you and my Godfather's work. I hope you aren't threatening me, cause if you are, you will be in prison for 15 years before the judge thinks about giving you probation and what do you think the public will think of you then? It would be like you never existed. My wife has the power and so do I. Your mother wouldn't give you a dime. Now, please leave my office. Mr. Ayes looks at Jon, but Jon didn't have a glimpse of hurt. Just boldness and no remorse. Mr. Ayes left. Oh. Mr.Ayes? Mr. Ayes: What?

Jon: Here are your divorce settlements. She will be getting married to your friend Micheally Sprinfield the reporter. Mr. Ayes: No, please! I'll do anything. Jon: You will be going back to your home in D.C., with your private plane. I'll give you that, free food on the plane and a 99 cent check. Good day! Jon says gentle with no anger. Mr. Ayes: Good Day, Sir. Jon watches Mr. Ayes as he walked away hitting his side thigh walking, Jon chuckles as he went back into his office. A note from the unknown was on his desk. A note and a box of candy and 5 wraps of $20 wrapped in rubber bands stacks of cash, bundle of money was flashing around with loose Diamond and Gold necklace. Jon looks with one eyebrow up as he hurried up and ran through the hall, Pounelle riding and riding, Jon runs down the stairs into the tracks he goes into, Pounelle stops at attention, Jon helps Pounelle down off the horse and gave her the Gold necklace from a person that didn't even have a name, we both smiles. Pounelle mind had a turn out, third eye turned green, her hands, cheeks and arms turned blue, eyes turned fire and fiercely open to her desire that was inside of her. Tears dried and hurt passed away by seconds and the gold was telling the heart win and prove. Jon: tonight is the derbey party, and I pray that you go. Pounelle: that party is for champions. Jon: you have to go, You are a champion, but you don't know it yet but once you'll see the children of Africa stand, show those bastards who they are doubting the wrong one. You have light and you shouldn't be ashamed to show it. Pounelle: if they keep killing the attendees, and keep destroying these women across the country to ride in the derbey, how many people do you think is going to bet on families that are losing? Jon: Power! Pounelle; Power? Jon: level of extensions. the question is someone outside is working inside, this business you don't know any extensions. Yang and King are looking outside. While Pounelle and Jon was talking on the tracks, Yang and King was listening to the heat of conversation, and they had cold blood shot red eyes that were painful. Pounelle stops talking as she looked, Contrnelle raised a fit and ran with Pounelle as Pounelle was being dragged across the track. Yang and King were smiling and laughing thinking they did the right thing, but they didn't. Pounelle didn't feel a thing, Jon and Contrnelle was right along on the side. Celsa? Jon called to the cloud as the cloud turned completely black as the horses eyes turned to fiercely black. Jon says a prayer to her Guardian Angel, mother Celsa (Jon) Dear Guardian Angel, please, watch over this child and protect her body and soul and let her not do what they do. Have her stronger and make her an eagle with wings that can race the destiny she wants and that she means to and let her do what she came her to do. Amen. Jon says last as he takes a deep breath into the rain that comes. Pounelle opened her eyes but not in position she thought she would be in, a tube acrossed her nose, needles in her veins and special rate normal. She looks around no one in the room. The doctors finally left when she woke up. Jon: How is she doc? Doctor: she came like an eagle that has wings, but it is hard to say about her brain, her brain expanded over night, her blood rushes fiercely and it is unstoppable, not only that her veins are as tight as a rock and we could hardly get in, the doctor here her breathing but she stops, Pounelle, stops her breathing, Pounelle goes back to flash, back with Contrnelle and remembers what was said her crown and third eye expanded and expanded and her veins started to grow and needles came out of one arm but she was still sleeping, they get pumpers and as they pumps thunder and lightning crashed light in the hospital. The light switched back on after dark occurred but as lights was off the memory of Contrnelle came to memory while Pounelle was on horse. Doctor: she strong everywhere, heart rate not normal, 999 of rate, veins outstanding, pulse 476 and mind rate 2,562. This champion is unbelievable. How does she manage? Sir, How do manage like this? is that your daughter? Jon: No, sir, She is is my wife and I manage real good and I let her be her. Doctor: Uh-huh, son, may I ask how old you are? Jon: I'm 15, Doc is something wrong? Doctor: Well, is your parents around? Jon: no sir, My mother Celsa died last week. Doctor: Celsa Venia? That was your mother? Jon: Yes, she was, and my dad is in Africa and. Doctor: well, who is with you? I am, a strange voice came behind Jon. Jon glances at his right shoulder, Godfather? Jon's Godfather was still alive and well at his age. Doctor: Vent Stone? Ahh, it is awesome to meet you, I heard you were a great poet of Italy. My father idolized you. Oh sign here please. How is business my son? Vent asked him as he grabbed his Godson and walks him outside and smokes his cigar. I heard about your your mother, I'm sorry, son, when I first seen your mother we were in Spain, we kept each other safe and then 5 years later I seen her again, she was carrying you. They both chuckles. I took back the company, Good! Vent said, joyful. It is your company, I don't want it. That is why I stayed away and dead all these years. What you heard was true. Your

Godmother died shortly after she let you go. She told you right, Charles Ayes was a sucker in grammar school had a lot of money, women houses at a young age. His father allowed him to have everything he wanted. My son, Jon. Let no evil come between you and that queen that is in there. You are a praying man. You have a company and a family. Let no evil, no evil come between you. What is going to happen no one in that international derbey is going to play fair. They are a crier for shame cause think insanity and braveness is the same thing, but it is not. Of what I seen you handled that meeting well. When you go to Texas tomorrow you make sure all eyes is on that beauty. Let fear come in between eyes of insanity. That queen is going to make a hit of glory. Glory and fame is two different things. My, son. You are a praying Godly man. Get to the point, Godfather Goodness, Always, throwing, alright, alright, alright, All I'm saying is, Let us not into temptation. Let no evil come between us. son. You choose right, my son. You treat that woman as your queen not your servant. Vent added as he walks back inside with his $94,876 silver and gold suit on, walking as he was actually known.

CHAPTER 14

CONTRNELLE AND THE DERBEY'S PALACE

Texas, October 2,2027 palace stadium was filled and Pounelle disappeared for months, no social media, no posts on social accounts, nothing came from Pounelle and Contrnelle was out of spotlight. Pounelle was in her locker room waiting for right time to show up and run in the derbey race. The way Pounelle felt fiercely ready to fly like an eagle, Pounelle sighs as she was looking at what Jon gave her closely to the mirror as her hair was short enough with day. Contrnelle was ready to back into the game. Reporters asking the riders about Pounelle being at the derbey but what are about to find out is shocking to the fans and to the riders. Jon just clapping and everyone is just surprised. Who are you clapping for? a woman asked with a little girl on the side of hand. Look mama! Everyone is screaming as they see Pounelle and Contrnelle coming towards the crowd as Pounelle was staring at Yang and King faking their true self. Pounelle? the reporters yells out as they seen Pounelle on the horse, looking closely to the eyes and the attention Contrnelle's eyes bend closely to the woman that made Pounelle angry. I see you are faking a stand, Pounelle says as she was circling Yang and King, three times and then stops after 4 turns, Yang shutters in reaction, I thought you were... Pounelle's eyebrows raised as she leaned over to the side gradually holding on the Contrnelle's head and letting the beauty know, go do your thing. Reporters: Any comments as all reporters are gathering around and leaving the others behind, Pounelle: everyone get ready Contrnelle will be champion and I will rule. I want light, cameras on whatever goes onto the other opponents, I want attention cause after Con wins again, I am sending everyone home with empty checkbooks, and no one will ever go against the greatest, ain't that right, Con? Contrnelle shook her head and eyed her other opponents that she knew that was not going to make it. Pounelle waves at the crowd and then steady the hors by grabbing the ebony hair and saying ready for destiny, going into the gates as she put on her goggles and ready to take over. In the lead with 50 points, Contrnelle in the lead with 60 points, crowd cheering for Contrnelle, North was screaming for Castle but both of East and West was cheering for Contrnelle while she was in the lead. Pounelle glances on both side of her shoulder and saw Yang and King on the side of Contrnelle, but Yang got in front blocking Contrnelle's view of getting the greatest object, Pounelle decided to take the lead but King has decided to grab Pounelle and yank but grief took over Pounelle, Pounelle kept an secret weapon in her pocket and cut King as King fell off the horse with a bloody cheek on her side, Pounelle kept on going, a lot of boos came in affect, Pounelle was just out of breath. It is alright Contrnelle, Pounelle sighed as she glanced at Jon and blows a kiss towards him. He smiles low, popcorn was thrown at them, what was that? Asol got in the middle and got punched by Pounelle, calm down Pounelle, they cheated and you are not Pounelle paused as she looked. Tomorrow you show them who England is but tonight they are not expelling you to be at the ball tonight. You hold the cards to this derbey and you show the world that you have everything, power glory, and potential. Ok. Jon. 3 hrs and a half time passed, Pounelle looked by the clock, 7:34 pm while Pounelle sits in the back of the bed wall staring at the black flat screen. Pounelle decides to skip ball for 2 hrs and walks inside a sparkling dress shop and gets a dress and walks to the dressing room and sizes her image with heels she picked smiles and holds her head high as she thinks and imagine Jon next to her with a smile. Maam? Pounelle points her fingers up. Yes, Miss? How much is this dress? This is fabulous. It is quite lovely, it is on the tag, Oh this is China's Boutique and it is $79,876. Ohhh, it is powerful! I'll take it, Pounelle says as she took off the dress, will that be cash or credit? Mrs. England? Credit, Pounelle answered with a smile. Here you are maam, will it be anything else? Yes, I want all the dress of China Boutique. All Maam? Yes, Maam, my credit card, Uh how old are you? nevermind, keept it, I'll take my money somewhere else. Macys, Ulta Beauty, Michael Kors, and everything you can think of. Subtotal $947,765,467.97, cash left trillions!!!! and more! Greatfully blessed! Pounelle said, closed. A hunk came by Mrs. England? Yes? I been requested to take you to the hotel that you are assigned to. Oh...Ok., as they arrived to the hotel, Pounelle hooked up her hair, toes, and everything was done. All she needed was her makeup and dress, all that was done in 55 mins. Pounelle was in the middle of Michael Kors or Nancy Gonalaz Clutch, she chose when Jon was at the door with a tailor made blue suit on. Pounelle opens and a smile came and peace did too. Jon presented his arm and closes the door with the other arm. As Jon and Pounelle Eageleton arrives at the Derbey carpet, says the reporter was saying in a distance. Everyone was silent as Jon and Pounelle was sharing a passionate kiss, while the lights were on them for 2 seconds. Jon allowed Pounelle to be as all reporteers were chatting to get the formers champions attention and Pounelle didn't hide from the lights, as a matter of fact, Pounelle endured it, Pounelle didn't mind the questions, the pictures, or the drama. Drama in the derbey was alright there, people dying to see Pounelle's next move but Pounelle's next move was vengeance.

CHAPTER 15

The bell rings as the horses ran a quarter mile, everybody rose to their feet when Contrnelle won the race and that 820 to one odd was the greeting to Pounell and Contrnelle. The beats was made with other professionals. The belief was no one studied Pounelle. Pounelle was in disguised and made an bet that Contrnelle would win over Castle and the worst part they did not know it was Pounelle making bets and signing contracts to take land and property on her. (Pounelle) I won everything, everyone was stunned to see me get the fame for everything they did not know, me and Jon was money happy but I had to get more than just money and power, I had to get my respect and without losing my dignity and my glory. Contrnelle was home with her family an in her country, I was praying to have freedom with strong maturity, power was one of my favorites that I have earned. $797,420, $994,762, and $444,766.96 and it totaled up at a large amount. Brokers came to my door and paid in cash in black suit cases. Jon chuckles at me while he touches money and sneaked some in, I hit his hand and he cried, I laughed at the fact that we were living off insanity and enemies but the main part was power and glory. Everything was in plan and love was between. Love and having power into a world that Contrnelle created by one beauty of confidence, when you are on the edge of abundance it creates confidence, love and power to run a race that you never expected, being able to look into an ebony beauty and see nothing but fire and spirit, you see you moving towards your will of fire. You hear trumpets in your ear, children chanting your name, waterfalls soothing in your brain and stallion running with your beauty, now can you call that a power of abundance? It has its own calling and so does abundance. As Jon, Contrnelle and I was on our own land in Spain, running our mansion and loving an adopted baby girl Melsa Eagleton England that was found on the acre that we lived on. No one claimed her for three weeks after reports were made. So, Melsa was ours for good. Our trip to the .S. was extremely different with a new born baby that was found in the England acres, that Jon and I brought together. As we arrived on the bus that we left England on, we both holding one end of the baby holder, all eyes came on us when we walked on the walkway, everybody off the bus Jon decided to walk up to the front and down the steps we go. As Jon was writing their last check, I glanced at Jon and Jon glanced at me, you recalled it and I am doing it, my heart pounded as he held my hand and extremely touches my lips with his pizza breath, I kissed fast.

Are you going to put us on the bus, man? Hold your breath, here is your check, so this is it? For me? Well, Uh.the point is Blena, Yeah, that is it for you? Blena tsks her teeth and folded her arms and stopped her feet as she cornered her eyes at Jon. Klemnta, here is your check. The derby final is three months away, and my father spent his money for my training and I promised I would finish this final. Pounelle approached Klemnta and looked into Klemnta's eyes, did you know about the cheating? Pounelle asked extremely to her, but Klemnta didn't answer. Did you? Yes or No? No answer. Remember, I told you I'm send your ass broke with my name across your back and I just didn't mean money. Pounelle twisted her wrist and then broke her nose. Pounelle turned back to Jon, Jon's mouth opened widely and others did too, so where were we? Pounelle says as she held Melsa in her arms with a blanket covering.

CHAPTER 16

Wednesday 16, 2027 October is when the horses was giving out horse autographs to fans, when I came to Contrnelle with Melsa in my arms, Melsa eyed her and Contrnelle felt tired but grounded. I felt all spirits come before us all, third eye started to open up. For weeks Contrnelle and I couldn't wake up, for a week as Pounelle was laying on the bed on her back, Melsa climbes on the stomach and sits there and does a prayer and then does a prayer position, chakra clearing in Pounelle's body took place, and at the same time Jon did the same thing to Contrnelle and both of them felt the changing of their own bodies, water rising tightly inside their minds, ears pumping, blood rushing to brain and pulse pumping. The baby decides to watch Pounelle's third eye, glow blossom. A memory of stallions came along to the room, it made clear, a knock came on the door. Pounelle! Pounelle! The guard got louder with the knocking. What? What? What? Pounelle yells as she opens the door with a smile, are you ready? asked her body guard Ashley. Ready? Ready for what? asked Pounelle. You have to meet your new opponents that just arrived and they look like killers. Pounelle glances over her shoulder and sighs, well so am I.

CHAPTER 17

The family arrives to see Jon and I after 8 months passed and in October 17, 2027 was when the family came, while we were out and about that is when I meet Vent, Jon's Godfather. He was amused to see what I looked like in person. Vent: I hoped you been treating this woman as your queen? Jon: Oh, I have, father, but she is a hard candy. Vent: of course she is, she will be champion, so what does champions get? Jon: The best. Vent: That's right! So, what is your trouble daughter? You having trouble getting your respect? Since Jon has been keeping your books since you were in the derby for 2 years, the scouts find you a threat to the derby International cause of your freedom and your youth, and you won the derby in 2022. I made the derby for the youth and it going quite well, this derby is not normal, you don't see 12 year olds on up. Pounelle: I want the respect that is due, I just won't get the respect cause I have money, I have to be champion to get the respect that I deserve. Money nor kindness will be the case, power. Will power be the case? Vent smiles and looks into her eyes, it is depending how you use it, you can misuse your power or you can use it right, it is your choice. You are older and stronger, you and Jon made this youth derby greater, but I hope you understand that this power is beyond me and this world, just remember, own it. Pounelle: own it? Vent: is something wrong about respect does not come easy, respect is like gold, you want the gold, but the level of stress is too high, it is like creating business, you want business but you don't have self-confidence. To ride Contrnelle, you can't be shy, you can't be insecure cause when that trumpet sound goes off, you gotta be tight with your stand. Stand is something that you have to have to win this derby, and this derby is not for education nor for the future, this derby is to each of its own. Most of the youth is not in it for education most of it is power and money. If you can be free into power you can be free in anything. I never did finish school, I stopped midway, I was homeschooled, I finished homeschooling and got my degree but I never did go to college, but my father left me plenty of money and gold, pearls and expensive jewels to sell that my father couldn't do. I am blessed to have freedom I just want my Godson to make the freedom I have, trillions of dollars in my name. Vent said in Pounelle's ear. My father left it for me, my mother left 999.9 pure 24 karat gold on my table and took me to the mountains and told me to leave only when I was 9. This is your derby, you are the one to make this happen. The next stage is, are you ready? Pounelle sighs as she folds her arm sitting on a black chair under the umbrella. So, what do you want to do? Proselluia asked with her white tips of her nails was tapping the table. I, I am still ready for the next five. Vent: are you ready? be ready and be fiercely powerful.

CHAPTER 18

I am sorry, her mother Proselluia started to say as she was peeling her fake nail, I am, I am really sorry that I doubted you and your decision, I was just trying to take my friend's advice about you riding Contrnelle, you and Contrnelle has been shaking the charts, you are all over the sports center news. I really wanted to change the hunger and let them be free, I hate the children that are hungry, I don't want that for them. I didn't grow up hungry, I didn't want them to be like me, I hat the fact that other children can have ipods and other things that children have. The women of society is so wrong, they just don't know a blessing of a horse, Contrnelle is a blessed champion, I just noticed how a 15 year old daughter is free to be her own woman, I let you go when I seen how you showed me how to be a woman and live in freedom and not allow others talks matter, around the neighborhood people shut their mouths to go to town, nobody was in town, they were all watching you and the other opponents. I am so proud of you! her mother Proselluia says holding her tightly in her arms. Mama, Jon and I have been married 7yrs and I love him. Proselluia chuckles, that explains the ring being on your finger for 7yrs. I don't care, baby girl, you have your own mind and you make your own decisions, who would know that you and Jon were meant for each other?! You are wonderfully blessed! Sometimes you take big risks, what is so wonderful is that you don't ask for a divorce. He is good to me mama! Pounelle exclaims! Jon traveled all the way from England to Africa just to meet me and he didn't know me, until I saw the photos of me and Jon. Contrnelle loves me and so does Jon. Pounelle? for real? Yes, look we sneak to take pictures, and get time in because he is running the derby. Whoa! Jon runs the derby? I do too but I decide to race. Proselluia and Pounelle runs to back to Jon, Mama, wait, I think my cornbread is on the table, Proselluia says running to Jon. Jon! Jon! Jon! Oh Lord, Jon says with a smile, Yes mama, Jon says laughing, hugging Pounelle with a tight sleeve. Where is Vent? I don't know, Pounelle. You are such a coco! Jon says kissing Pounelle with melted strawberry dip on his lips. ha! Yay! Vent says coming in the middle of the street with Contrnelle and two officers, it is 2027, live your champion life up. Jon was the first one to clap and cheer for her to get on the horse, Contrnelle rises up to the sun and stays up for a couple of mins and meets Pounelle's third eye.

CHAPTER 19

The crowd gets louder as Pounelle was signing people's autographs, a throat clears in the back of Pounelle. Uh, huh? Pounelle sighs in the middle of the sentence, you must be the new heifer I going to face, that is correct, you need, No, I think you need to know my name. My name is Pounelle England Eagleton, Jon's wife, that's right. My name is Trutheya Augustinaa and I am here to take you out Pounelle England. I rather strike out cause your paycheck is going to have a strike of blood on the side. Don't ever, I mean ever, interrupt my fun with my fans, you show me some respect, you hear me? Pounelle says with her hand over her hip. Augustinaa: Oh, Pounelle, why are you here? Pounelle: the question is for you, why are you here? Augustinaa: that is a question on top of a question, and I am not that dumb. I am very smart. Pounelle chuckles and swirl her long red hair down her chin. Augustinaa: what type of hairstyle is that anyway? Short in the back and a bang in the front. Pounelle: a style of freedom, that is the style I have, and besides the way I dress, walk and talk have power, and if you are smart, then why are you such a bitch about a person that has more freedom than you? No answer came from Augustinaa, she walks away with an ugly humor. A fan was eyeing Pounelle as she was signing autographs for fans once more, and taking photos of them all together, all eyes on

Pounelle, and Pounelle was having fun with the babies, just like the fans were having fun with Pounelle. Rain drops started to fall, and Pounelle asked did you feel that? Pounelle glanced at the sky, and smile, more rain sprinkles came down from the sky as Pounelle stood there and let the rain hit her skin and her hair, the working hands of a woman and the style of grace. The horses was frightened and ran back to their owners, but Contrnelle was blessed to thunder of the sound. The sound of conquer this and become this. (Pounelle) The part of conquering was the hardest but remembering the words that was bestowed upon me was "Rain is the power of your name and your name is the power of the rain. That was the power source of it all. I was ready for vengeance but instead I want to be remembered of the daughter champion not the vengeance of fear, madness or hate. Just power and respect of destinies. I certainly want power but not justice, certainly want lover but not frightened passion. The status was part of my name, love and passion in between for Jon was created roughly cause we were forced into marriage by my father's signature in China, then war started. 7 years later we reconnected and stronger than ever. 2012 was the adorable time, but now it time for power. I am ready for the knocks, the spits the hate and madness that come towards this power. I be ready to feed the bullshit that opponents give to get the power that is mines. I hope they know what they are getting themselves into, cause I am all game.

Chapter 20

No Problem Mrs. Eagleton

Inside the Derbey International came Pounelle England Eagleton into the building with her long green party dress, red lip gloss, and pink eyeshadow. Hello, Micheally, Hello Mrs. Eagleton. Mrs. Eagleton your non alchol wine. Oh thank you. Pounelle: Ha! What's ya name? You on the corner. Name? Staylla Willde 3 yr in Willits CA. Pounelle: what is your horse's name? Opponent: Dahey Willde. Pounelle: hmm, pretty, you're in, so sign up over there. I am only going to pick 5 and that is it. The rest of you that thought I deal with you later. The rest go sign except for you 8, you are not welcomed back to this derby at all. So thank you for coming down here, and for your time. I really thank you. If there is any, I mean any certain problem, you can come to me and talk. Mrs. Eagleton? Pounelle: Yes? Mrs. Eagleton, I know you are the boss and everything, but you are not fair. Pounelle: excuse me? listen, you don't come around me and talk your innocent bullshit around me like you are a God. You are nothing comparing to where I am standing, you are no different than the people that dies on that field each day, they are important just as well as you, so you think you can take a risk getting on that horse and looking deep inside yourself and take the risk that others took? You brave enough? Take your lead, but until then stay out of my way. Here are the paperworks for everything that you may need, here is the contract to sign, just in case you get hurt or injured, here is your documents. Why do take big risks? Mrs. Eagleton? Pounelle: If you have it in you to do this do it, cause once you sign this there is no going back. Do you want to do this? Yes or No? Don't worry about me and why I take big risks, cause I watch my own back I don't need you to watch it for me, I take risks cause I love the horses and this aint no play thing with me. There are people on that field that don't care about your innocent bullshit, and what you think you deserve, and that includes me.

CHAPTER 21

Pounelle greeted the new corners that was signed in. Yang: they all looked so scared and innocent like they have not taken big risks, see you are so young and I am going to make an example out of Pounelle.

Pounelle: Hey Yang, you forgot I don't have the look of innocence on my face like these young women here, you forgets that I sent your ass home broke, Pounelle says, as she looks at the board on top of the timer, "that's me", and these women they have not taken risks like I have, you cheating bitch. Ladies, don't forget when you take risks out here tonight just remember a cheater never gets power, its the winners that get the glory, not losers that can't win without taking down the gold brick without crashing it, meaning if you cheat, you are a loser. Yang: don't push it. Pounelle: Don't worry I am not the one that is pushing 50, seems like you are, cause for all I can see is that you are going to have a bloody nose with my name all over you. Yang: Just keeping pushing it. Staylla: What does that mean? Wh-What have you gotten us into? We are...In a battlefield. Staylla says dramatically, Oh my God. Pounelle: Just relax, you are the one wanted to do this and now have this opportunity don't be afraid of it, you wanted this, you got it, if you stick with this for 2 yrs, you will $656,000 a yr, that is the new income. Staylla: and if we lose? Pounelle: You are not going to get the same income like you would if you win, you don't get paid to lose, you get paid to win. If you get passed the society level. Staylla: What do you mean Society level? Pounelle chuckles, you will see when you get out there. Don't look so shocked, don't ask for anything that you don't understand, see you tonight! Pounelle glances at them and then looked at her watch, the derby won't start until 2 hours. While the wind started to blow hardly to the bare skin of everyone, Pounelle breezes in the air as she goes down the derby palace ramp. She gasps and right then and there Yang confronted her, close and person, eye to eye. Who do you think you are? I am Pounelle England, not Eagleton, not Gableton, but just England and I am a winner, always will be. Yang: you listen to me you old rotten fashion, I am champion all over my world, so you better watch it. Pounelle: You might be all over the world, but you are nothing in this world, this right here, is my world, Pounelle's world, and you haters are just crawling to get to my skin, trying to eat something sweet but when you are in my world its sour, and if you can't live up to my world then you better leave now. Yang: What about the new opponents that you allowed in?

Pounelle smiles and does not answer, just walks away and then turns around and says what are going to do? Yang gave an aggressive look, bring it in one hour. Pounelle closes her eyes and towards the wall her fingers touched the paint that was wet. Pounelle quickly got up looked at the side of her shoulder. Pounelle gasps, Mr. Ayes, What are you doing in the back of me? What do you want? Here is something for protection, you will need it. For? Mrs. Ayes cut her palm of her hand deeply into her veins and gets it out. Pounelle watches closely to what she was saying as the blood non stop came from her palm, Mrs. Ayes, Pounelle whispers. Shh, this is what is going on her, this is what is out there on that field tonight, grief and conquer. Conquer this Pounelle and you will have the world at your toenails. Crowd is cheering for you, Pounelle. Is it passed one hr? Pounells says as she walks in the crowd, jogging her way down with the horse, Pounelle glancing at the crowd and the expression on their faces, to be exposed into this international derby. Pounelle takes a sigh and entered the gate, turns and look over her shoulder and sees a spiritual angel on side and in front, her hands turning blood shot red and her skin turning hard with white veins, and heart and soul, mind with all hurting with all minders. Pounelle's ears rang with a tone and a memory of the white stallion horses. The trumpet bell rings and all the horses ran but Pounelle stood still and glances to the crowd, angles leading my eyes to Jon grabbing the knife peeling an apple looking at Pounelle with a non to consider, a cruel look came on Jon's face and as it he saw the crowd move Pounelle took at the glance of the other horses. The angeles took wings and flew over the head of Contrnelle and Contrnelle took charged and ran. (Pounelle) the angels were in the crowd but the moment took affect of us, as the other horses were darkened into harsh energy, but as we conquered, we have received our destiny of being us and no one could take it. The lives that we see are taken but the eyes of others, no once can change or become me. Wind blows, heart stops, mind wonders clearly but the dreams come from within.

CHAPTER 22

(Pounelle)

The moves when you take your wings and put it into the other but once and for all someone taught me how to accept destinies and manage them into your own and that was an angel that comes to affect and as we speak the universe will realize how strong the world is with one accord. That day day we became champions to each other and willing to take our destinies to the next level. The eyes of champion is the eyes of Contrnelle. Free-will is to take others down one by one and let them understand the change by winning and having power over other as they choose to be ignorant into my way of freedom. P. S. No one will win until the will of freedom take its power. Pounelle England

Printed in the United States
By Bookmasters